For Leia Martine Banker, with love from your dadu!
Ashok

To my dark chocolatey brown Thatha (grandfather),
for having brought endless laughter, drama and delight.
Sandhya

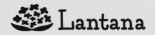 Lantana

I am BROWN

Written by
ASHOK BANKER

Illustrated by
SANDHYA PRABHAT

I am brown

I am beautiful

I am perfect

I am love

I am friendship

I am happiness

I am
a doctor

a lawyer

a writer

an astronaut

an athlete

a scientist

an actor

an electrician

a president

a prime minister

a singer

I make art

I design rocket ships

I code computers

I build houses

I come from

Chinese   Spanish   French   English

Marathi   Swahili   Japanese   German

Arabic   Russian   Indonesian   Tamil

black hair

brown hair

no hair

black eyes

green eyes

brown eyes

I live in

a cottage

a house

an apartment

a mansion

a riverboat

a hut

a bungalow

a cabin

I eat

noodles

tacos

samosa

vindaloo

biryani

steak

tagliatelle

jhal
muri

barbecue

fattoush

I wear
a shirt and
a jacket

a top and
a skirt

a blouse and
a saree

a salwar and
a kameez

a shirt and
a lungee

a business
suit

a kurta and
a dhoti

a prom
dress

a wedding
gown

a lehenga

your boss

your driver

your teacher

your guru

5 + 3 =

I pray at

a temple

a church

a mosque

a synagogue

everywhere

a shrine

a dargah

a gurdwara

nowhere

I am brown   I am amazing

I am YOU

First published in the United Kingdom in 2020 by Lantana Publishing Ltd., London.
www.lantanapublishing.com

American edition published in 2020 by Lantana Publishing Ltd., UK.
info@lantanapublishing.com

Reprinted in 2020

Distributed in the United States and Canada by Lerner Publishing Group, Inc.
241 First Avenue North, Minneapolis, MN 55401 U.S.A.
For reading levels and more information, look for this title at www.lernerbooks.com
Cataloging-in-Publication Data Available.

Printed and bound in China.
Original artwork created digitally.

ISBN hardcover: 978-1-911373-94-0
ISBN eBook PDF: 978-1-911373-96-4
ISBN ePub trade: 978-1-913747-12-1
ISBN ePub S&L: 978-1-913747-38-1